The Lion Gods of Destiny

The Blood of The Gods

The Lion Gods of Destiny

The Blood of The Gods

Mackenzie C. R. Williams

ASA PUBLISHING CORPORATION
AN INNOVATIVE OUTSOURCE BOOK PUBLISHING HYBRID

Advancing Trust Together℠

ASA Publishing Corporation
An Accredited Hybrid Publishing House with the BBB
www.asapublishingcorporation.com
29 S. Monroe St., Suite 201, Monroe, Michigan 48161

Copyrights© 2022, Mackenzie C. R. Williams, All Rights Reserved
Book Title: The Lion Gods of Destiny *The Blood of The Gods*
Date Published: 03.28.2022
Edition: 1, *Trade Paperback*
Book ID: ASAPCID2380828
ISBN: 978-1-886528-59-8
LCCN: Cataloging into Publication

This book was published in the United States of America.
Great State of Michigan

Table of Contents

The Lion Gods of Destiny

The Blood of The Gods

SUMMARY

The Lion God Aalam king of the gods had four sons. Adel the god of Justice is the first born, Abner the god of Light is the second born, Aksel the god of Peace is the third born, and the fourth son born was Aaru the god of Harmony.

All the realms were in order, and peace was among many worlds until his first born turned dramatically evil because he thought that his father betrayed him when he overheard him secretly announcing one of his brothers as future king of heaven.

This is how the legend of *The Blood of the Gods* begins.

THE BOX

The box is known to be an old ancient forbidden living relic eons ago; during the darkness before the worlds were ever formed. No planet was in existence, only the gods and this ancient evil that existed when battling over the universe among the realms.

This box, sealed by the gods who trusted the Lion God Aalam and the generations of forefathers before him in his lineage. Now Lion God Aalam is protected against this box, but others are not void from it. The harnessed entity inside the box corrupts the mind, it picks its host by a blinding madness. It only chooses the most vulnerable and acceptable being of extraordinary power, it will either consume its host or destroy the host if it is in questionable rejection by crystallization and soon with disintegration.

This box is alive, a living being of unsurmountable evil that lives on the skirts of the god realms.

INTERLUDE

One day Adel discovered this ancient forbidden box in the weapons chamber between two gargoyle statues that protects it from any intruder trying to open it.

"Hum, what's this?" Adel reaching in between the statues.

"No, don't, . . . stop!" his father yells as he looks up into the realms while watching his son's arm penetrating through the blue forcefield in between the gargoyles.

ARC 1

In the beginning . . .

Within the king of the gods, Aalam is the great-great grandson of the former King Ara his great-great grandfather.

When Ara was King, he fought a very

powerful and an omnipotent evil being known as Azazel. When the battle was over and the ancient one was defeated, he was sealed away in a box to keep his evil from spreading across the universe. Having defeated this evil, King Ara was kept with the responsibility of making sure that the seal will never be broken.

After a hundred years had passed, this responsibility was given to his son Adelio who would be Aalam's great grandfather, then Aalam's father King Abban, and soon then Aalam the new King of the gods.

Trumpets were sounding and cheers was roaring throughout the city gates as King Aalam comes home from another glorious battle on a white Pegasus with strong forces behind him. The majestic arch angels, wings stretching across the sky and making way through a vast ocean of clouds as they reached the kingdom of heaven; the kingdom of the gods. It was during the time when his children were very young.

Settling in on his throne he calls his four boys to present them with various gifts. When his oldest begin to approach his father King Aalam, the king knew immediately that something wasn't right, that he sensed a present danger within him, not at yet knowing what it is, or what it was about. All he knew is somehow a dark presence of old will be looming over his son, and that the realms will be in grave danger.

"What's wrong, Father?" as Adel the *god of Justice* the first born tries to extract the gift out of his father's hands.

"Oh, nothing. Excuse me son . . . (loosening his grip) where are my manners." Staring at Adel again with concern and trying to shake off the imbalanced expression. "Here you go, son."

"Thanks, Father."

"Now for the rest of you, come on up here!"

As everyone stands up, the King then walks away heading toward his chamber, still having this thought of darkness that might somehow consume his oldest son in the near future.

While in his chamber, the King begins

pacing frantically back and forth, contemplating what to do about the situation that he and the Kingdom of Heaven might face. Still standing, his palms pressing on the top of the desk, staring into the mirror as visions begins to run wildly through his mind.

King Aalam immediately jumps back and yells, "ENOUGH!!! . . . I shall not let this evil consume my son!" Then he calls out to the guards.

"Guards, Guards, Guards!"

The King then goes to open the door as he hears the light fist pounding sound of his guard's armor.

"We're here, Sir!"

"Oh, yes of course, do come in."

"How may we be of an assistance, your Highness?"

"Go to the armory and check the box."

Both guards looked at each other in puzzlement, then one turned toward King Aalam, as the nervousness begins to creep across the hairs on the back of his neck.

"But your highness, no-one has ever dared to come close to it in over a 1,000 years."

"Yes, I know, but do as I command. I need you to tell me what you see once you're there, but please do not touch anything."

Again, both guards turned back toward each other in fear that they may never return again, because of the legend that was told throughout history about this mystical box.

"But, Sir?"

"Did you not just hear me! . . . GO!!!"

The guards nodded and went to do as instructed.

ARC 2

-*The Apparition of Adel* -

Adel looking at his father in bewilderment, shook his head from side to side, thinking that his father has probably lost his mind and perhaps needed some rest. But, what no-one knows as of yet, it has already happened.

"Thank you for the gift, father."

"You're quite welcomed, my son."

And as soon as King Aalam reaches up to touch the shoulders of his son in gratitude on each side while staring into his eyes, he saw a very dark image of his son's shadow on the wall behind him moving on its own for a few quick seconds. Immediately, King Aalam violently yanked his hands off his son's shoulders.

"Father, what's wrong? Why did you snatch your hands away from me? Are you ill?"

King Aalam, yet, was left so speechless, that he backed up holding his chest with his left hand gasping for air, as though he was choking, and had his right arm extended, making clear evidence to his son, that he do not want to be touched. But, his son kept on moving forward to aid in helping his father, although King Aalam still refused to let his son touch him.

"Father, why don't you let me help you? Are you okay?! . . . Father . . . Father! Please, . . . tell me what's wrong!"

"Uh, I'm okay now, son. You go on, I'll be alright."

"Are you sure?"

"Yes, my son. I just need to lay down a little bit. You go on, now."

Just as his son, Adel was exiting the chamber, in comes between them only one of the guards that the King sent on an errand mission.

"Sir! . . ."

"Not now – not now!" waving his hand at the guard telling him to just back off at the moment.

#####

Unfortunately, it did consume him. The shadow of the son is the visualization evidence that demonstrates the beginning of the consumption. When Adel hears and starts listening to the voices, that will be the beginning of a growing destructive force within him; a changeover that could soon destroy the universe.

After Adel's father, Aalam knew of this ancient evil within his son; the darkness of old that revealed itself, the king felt its presence growing stronger and stronger as Adel innocently walked out without knowing that bit-by-bit, the evil will begin chipping away at destroying his mind, tearing the very fabric of his god-like conscience. It will speak to him and kill his heart with bitterness, hatred, and anger towards his brothers that his father, King Aalam adored so much. This his father had seen in the premonition that he wished would not come to past, but it was already too late. Adel, now in his room having great thoughts about being king and wanting nothing more than to sit on the throne.

King Aalam prior knew that his son, Adel wasn't ready to become king, and had secretly left this private decision between Adel's younger brothers without his acknowledgment. Yet, while Adel was sitting down in his room, the whispers in his mind told him to take a walk to the garden.

This is where the collision takes place. His brothers were already there; altogether, laughing and gesturing around, talking about how each one, if they were to become king what they would do.

When Adel reached the garden, he saw his brothers congregating together; seems like they were having a good ole time. Instead of interrupting, he decided to listen in. When Adel was listening, he heard them talk about becoming king.

The second born son. "When I am

king, I'm going to bring love and happiness across the universe."

The third born son. "When I become king I will give all my gold to the homeless and feed the hungry."

When Adel overheard his brothers talking about what they would do if they were king, the darkness inside Adel began twisting his mind into plotting against his brother, and his father as well.

"Auh, man! No . . . No-No, No-No, . . . No! This can't be happening to me! I mean, . . . how could they? Why? Why me?! I just can't believe they would betray me like this. Those BASTERDS!!!" awkwardly yelling he is running off down the corridor, out and away from the garden.

As Adel was panicking frantically through this frustration, the darkness enjoyed absorbing much of it, and withdrawed from a lighter shade of Adel's innocence to a darker shade of madness.

"Hey younger brother, did you hear something?" questioned Abner.

"No, I'm not sure. But I wish our older brother was here to tell us what his thoughts and feelings are about becoming king."

Yeah, if dad changes his mind. By-the-way, dad has been acting a little funny lately. Have you noticed?" chimed in, Aaru.

Lateron that evening, Adel began devicing a plot to stop his father's plans of wanting to make one of his brothers becoming king. So, Adel created a way to deceive his father's soldiers to follow him and started a revolutionary war from the inside, a coup; an overthrow of his father's kingdom.

Adel continues to gather more followers by day through the exercising of his enormous strength that has been empowered by the darkness that is within him. This evil that lies inside continues to grow, making Adel much more smarter and agile. This also adds to the blinding of his father's foresight to see in the many different realms of the future, allowing Adel's agility to perform this unwanted hostile takeover.

Adel was becoming more and more corrupt by this old ancient evil, telling him to be higher than his father, whispering, "Adel, you can be more powerful than your father ever could. You can rule over the earth, the heavens, and even the universe. All you have to do is kill your brothers and you're your father. Then, and only then, you can become the Ruler Supreme . . ."

"KILL THE GODS!!! And sit on your father's throne!"

Unknown to the naked eye, Adel is actually fighting within himself waging war in his mind against the evil that has consumed him, not letting his conscious go. But, as a god himself, subconsciously, his memories are an essense of his forefathers that have been emplanted for such a time as this. Never-the-less, this type of strength cannot penetrate this internal madness, for Adel is the god of Justice, and the evil within is harnessing it with life-long vengeance against all who imprisoned him.

ARC 3

-The Plot of Chaos-

In the beginning before everything was, and, before there was even a thought, the universe burst into exisitence. As time went on and light began to illuminate its glory throughout the plains of this vast darkness, there arose mighty kings; gods of the absolute. Fierce warriors. But, only one can rule the universe. And so it shall . . . a Lion God King emerging between the realms, separating light from darkness, good from evil, justice and equality from anarche and deception. He was powerful, strong, and also fierce, yet created with passion. Among the others, evil reared its head as a jealous defeated god, an entity known as Azazel.

No, Azazel was not like the others, his heart was as black as the darkness fed its appetite for savagery and bloodthirsty violence. He would not accept defeat, he swore an oath to himself that one day he will be ruler of the universe, including the realms in which they reside.

Over ten millenniums has past, and the birth of humankind was left into the gentle hands of the Lion God King; teaching, nurturing, and cultivating them and their civilization. Soon the humankind; humanity and other gods began to worship this kind and gentle King of the gods, unknowing that an evil presence is still lerking beyond the stonewalls of his new-found kingdom.

The universe has been kind to the Lion God King Ara, and blessed him with a son for keeping the peace among the universe, it's realms, and the worlds within them. However, Azazel, also being the king's brother, was not pleased, continually grew bitter and envious.

#####

The god Azazel was an enuyness god and hated his brother the royal heir to the Lion God Throne; being a jeaous god Azazel, grew tired of his brother being better than him in every way making him bitter. Azazel, as the second born son he was always being told that he was meant for greatness by his mother. Azazel plotted against his brother Ara, so he can take the throne and rule over all things and damned anyone who were against him, so he banned with the god Loki.

Loki being the god of Mischief, Azazel knew he was clever and that he knew his way around, so they both came up with a plan to take the Lion God Throne. But Loki was a clever god; also very treacherous. Loki knew of Azazel's hatred for his brother the king. Staying in the shadows, Loki planned to betray Azazel but in doing so he had to tread carefully for Azazel. He was not just the king's brother, but Azazel was the god of Light and Power, and he was far more powerful than him. Loki being the worse god makes Azazel's position of a higher rank than loki, himself. So then on, Loki and Azazel teamed up to take the kings place by creating a powerful weapon with the gods of darkness.

It was just a matter time . . .

ARC 4

-The Blood of The Gods-

The Lion God King Ara ruled over everything, even the gods and their realms. Being the first born son and God King over everything and in each kingdom, and their worlds along with being ruler over mankind, he spread blessings upon blessings over the realms and brought peace, but he knew that his brother grew enuyness of him.

Being king came first and he had to protect his kingdom from treasons, for he also knew that he had to put an end to his brother's devilish plans; that his brother is mentally saturated with envy, the Lion God is also filled with a deep sadness for his family. And in doing so, it leaves a hole in his heart. But the Lion God King knows that he must stop this madness, for there is no time to weep.

So the gods and goddess of each realm prepared themselves for war in order to stop this evil from taking over. Odin, Athena, Thor, and many more of their brother and sister gods alike.

As the gods of the *realms of light* are preparing for war, the gods of darkness plan to takeover the Lion God's realm by using their dark powers to create a weapon of mass distruction, calling it the Cord of Chaos. The gods of evil created this string of power which was made by the fabric of dark energy and the blood of the god Azazel. By using his blood, Azazel could control the cord at will, obeying his every command.

What such weapontry the gods of darkness created; such a weapon as this being able to kill the most powerful god in the universe, targeting the Lion God King, the goddess, and the other gods of light. Even within the same powerful energy corrupting the realms, and leaving nothing left but mankind bowing down before them as slaves to do Azazel's bidding.

With the gods of the realms of light preparing for war, they too have created a weapon like no other; creating a box - a *Holy Crator* that can seal away evil. They call this weapon the Holy Trinity of Zion. This weapon will stop the gods of darkness, including the Lion God Ara's brother, Azazel. By being able to activate this device Odin, Zeus, Thor, and Athena used their blood along with the Lion God King's blood, giving it great-great power. It was by their godly blood, and through the Lion God King who used his ominipentent power to make this creation strong enough that not even the most powerful god could ever break open the seal. Now, the battle was upon them. So, the gods and goddess got ready for war; for they heard the horn of battle.

ARC 5

-War of the Realms-

After the gods had finished creating this containment box, the Lion God King asked the gods of the realms of light the power to aid him in the fight to stop this evil. But then, the trumpet of war was sounded and the kingdom of the Lion God and the other gods got ready to fight for the throne as with the gods of darkness coming with their warriors.

Azazel boasted, "I have come to take my rightful place as king of the realms, so make way for the true king!"

The gods and goddess of realms of light began getting into position. Thor with his hammer along with six million warriors were armed and ready as the Lion God King responded, and what he said was this, "Hear me, for I am the god of this realm and you shall not pass. I am the true and mighty king and I am the ruler of all the realms."

As the Lion God spoke these words it

angered Azazel, and as it did the battle for the realms began. The heavens and the universe was in a uproar, the battle raged on and there was great bloodshed. Many was lost, including the gods and goddess, or the lights of lights same, were destroy, and their blood stained the ground. But, for the gods of darkness most of them were also killed leaving only Loki and Azazel left in the battle. But Loki was a coward and betrayed Azazel by turning against him and killing off their own gods of darkness as well. And it raged Azazel; furiated him, killing Loki.

As the battle continued, Azazel was going up against his brother. Azazel trying to use the dark core that he created again was destroyed. For it was no match for his brother's holy powers. Azazel was defeated and sealed away to pay for his sins, trapping him in the box, the Holy Crator, for all eternity; trapped forever in this holy prison and locked by the gods of the realms of light. So the Lion God King banished the rest of gods of darkness into the dark abyss from where he came from, for Azazel lost the war, vanquished in a sealed box, never to return again.

Once the battle has ended the Lion God put the box in his weapons vault sealing his brother for all eternity, and the blood of the Lion God King will live on forever. When the war for the kingdom had ended and the god Azazel was sealed away, the lost was great for the gods of the realms of light who had won the fight. So they sworn vengeance, then sang and made music, but Lion God King Ara was sad, for he had lost a brother. But even through the loss of his brother and that his soul was evil, in doing so, he had to think of the next generations because he had a great-great grandson named Aalam who will be next line heading towards the throne of the Lion God King. In this way his highness's blood and linage will continue on. For they are the righteous and just, they are the keepers of light.

After the former Lion God Ara saved the universe from his brother and sealed him away for all eternity, time had passed, and the new generations were becoming of age where Ara's great-great grandson, Aalam had finally made it a step away closer to the throne of the Lion God King, his great-great grandfather.

Now being the new God King, Aalam had to carry his great-great grandfather's legacy and all that he had done to protect and pass along to the next following generation for the kingdom. But, this time not only did he have a son, but four sons, one being the elder son, Adel. A young future god king that had a very long ago hardened and angry spirit; cursing the kingdom and his family. It was heartbreaking that God King Aalam had to stop his first born son from taking over his kingdom, knowing with god-like vision of sight, that once the young boy was consumed by the evil in the box that his great-great grandfather had sealed away, the universe will be once more in danger again. But can the gods of this generation be able to stop the ancient darkness of old?

To Be Continued . . .